How many *Fairy Animals* books have you collected?

- Chloe the Kitten
- Bella the Bunny
- Paddy the Puppy
- Mia the Mouse
- Hailey the Hedgehog
- Sophie the Squirrel
- Poppy the Pony
- Betsy the Bunny
- Daisy the Deer
- Katie the Kitten
- Polly the Puppy
- Paige the Pony

Fairy Animals

of Misty Wood

Paige the Pony

Lily Small

EGMONT

With special thanks to Thea Bennett.

EGMONT
We bring stories to life

Paige the Pony first published in Great Britain 2015
by Egmont UK Limited
The Yellow Building, 1 Nicholas Road
London W11 4AN

Text copyright © 2015 Hothouse Fiction Ltd
Illustrations copyright © 2015 Kirsteen Harris Jones

ISBN 978 1 4052 7663 4

www.egmont.co.uk
www.hothousefiction.com
www.fairyanimals.com

A CIP catalogue record for this title is available from the British Library.

Printed and bound in Great Britain by The CPI Group.

59591/1

MIX
Paper
FSC FSC® C018306

Contents

CHAPTER ONE
Midsummer Morning

It was the most beautiful morning
in Misty Wood, and the sun was
shining high in the sky. Down
in the luscious green meadow, a

little silver Petal Pony was leaping about excitedly. It was the day of the Midsummer Pony Gala, the most wonderful fairy-pony show of the year!

Paige the Petal Pony kicked her heels high in the air and neighed happily. 'I can't believe it's finally here,' she said to herself, feeling the warm sunlight on her back. 'The day of the Pony Gala, at last!'

Paige was so excited that she couldn't sit still. She'd been waiting for this special day all summer. She galloped over the grass, her pretty silvery-grey coat a blur in the sunshine.

She raced right around the meadow three times. She could have kept running all morning! But then she heard someone calling her name. 'Paige!' came her mum's voice. 'Where are you?'

Paige skidded to a halt. 'I'm here, Mum!'

Paige's mum trotted over to the middle of the field. 'You're up very early, little one,' she said, nuzzling Paige hello.

'The Prettiest Pony Competition is tonight,' Paige said happily. 'It's always my favourite part of the Gala, and I finally get to compete this year. So I've got to practise my circles!'

MIDSUMMER MORNING

Then Paige leapt in the air and set off faster then ever.

Her mum laughed. 'You're making my head spin! You know the Prettiest Pony Competition isn't a race, don't you?'

Paige slowed to a trot, huffing and puffing to catch her breath. Well, *that* was true. She remembered all the beautiful ponies trotting and cantering in circles last year, and leaping over

6

the show jumps. None of them had galloped.

Paige stood still for a moment in the warm breeze, remembering how wonderful last year's Gala had been. She was sure this year's would be even better.

'Phew,' Paige's mum said, a twinkle in her eye. 'I couldn't think straight with you rushing round in circles like that.'

Paige trotted over and

snuggled up close to her mum.
'What's *your* favourite part of the
Gala?' she asked.

Her mum looked thoughtful.
'I do love the showjumping. Your
dad will be one of the judges this
year. Long ago, before you were
born, he was the champion showjumper!'

'Really?' said Paige, her eyes
wide. 'Ooh, I wonder if I could be
a champion showjumper too.'

8

She bounded over to a big thistle plant and tried to jump over it. But Paige was only a little Petal Pony, and she didn't quite make it. 'Ouch!' she squeaked, as the prickles scratched her leg.

Her mum chuckled. 'Maybe you can try the show jumps next year, when you're a bit bigger.'

'Yes, I will,' said Paige, instantly forgetting the scratch on her leg. 'But this year, I'm going

to try for the Prettiest Pony.'

She pranced happily around the meadow, lifting her knees as high as she could. 'Look at me! I hope the judges think I'm pretty.'

Paige's mum nodded. 'The judges will certainly notice a fine trot like that. But . . .'

'But what, Mum?' Paige said, as she whirled round in a perfect pirouette.

'. . . the judges will also be

looking for the pony with the shiniest coat, the softest mane, the silkiest tail and the brightest hoofs,' said her mum with a smile. 'Not to mention the kindest heart.'

Paige stopped in her tracks, and looked down at her pearly hoofs. There were grass stains on them, from all the galloping.

She shook out her snowy mane. There were quite a few

tangles in it. She turned her head to see her coat. It was dusty with grass seeds, from where she had stretched out on the ground to sleep last night.

Last of all, Paige swished her tail. It was full of pollen from all the flowers that grew nearby.

Uh-oh. Paige was a mess!

'What shall I do?' she said, worried. 'I'm not very shiny or soft or silky or bright at all.'

MIDSUMMER MORNING

Paige's mum nuzzled the little pony. 'You always look pretty to me, Paige. But if you want to look your best for the Gala, why don't you trot over to Heather Hill? You could roll in the heather to make your coat shine.'

'What a good idea!' Paige said. 'And I can do my special job, as well.'

All the fairy animals in Misty Wood had special jobs. The Petal

14

Ponies' job was to flick their tails over the flowers, wafting their beautiful scent into the air for the other fairy animals to enjoy.

'Are you coming too?' Paige asked her mum.

'No, I'll stay here,' her mum replied. 'Your little sister, Pia, will be waking up any minute. But you'll be fine. Off you go and have some fun.'

The two of them rubbed noses

to say goodbye, and then Paige set off for Heather Hill.

As she cantered over the meadow, a head bobbed up from the long grass. It was Petey the Pollen Puppy. 'Want to have a race?' he barked.

'Sorry, Petey,' Paige said, slowing down. 'I've got to get ready for the Pony Gala.'

'Good luck,' Petey said, wagging his tail. 'See you there!'

16

'See you!' Paige flicked her mane and raced on.

As she came to the edge of the wood, Daisy the Dream Deer bounded out of the trees. 'Good morning, Paige!' she called, in her soft voice. 'Did you have sweet dreams last night?'

'Hello, Daisy,' Paige called. 'I did! I dreamed about the Pony Gala. I'm entering the Prettiest Pony Competition!'

17

Some other Dream Deer came leaping to join Daisy. 'We hope you win,' they cried.

'We love the Gala!' And they bounded off into the wood again.

Suddenly there was a rustle by Paige's feet, and she jumped in surprise. A pile of leaves on the ground stirred and two beady eyes peeped up at her.

It was Mia the Moss Mouse. 'Hello, Paige,' Mia squeaked. 'I thought I heard thunder, but it was just your hoofs drumming on the ground.'

'I'm hurrying to get ready for the Pony Gala,' Paige explained. 'I'm sorry if I frightened you.'

'Ooh, I love the Pony Gala,' Mia said, twitching her whiskers. 'Good luck!'

Paige cantered on through

the trees until she came out on the
other side of Misty Wood – and
there was Heather Hill!

'Mmm,' Paige sighed, as she
breathed in the lovely scent of the
purple heather flowers.

She flicked her tail over the
flowers a few times, sending the
scent into the air for the other
fairy animals to enjoy. Then she
lay down and rolled over and over
on the bouncy bushes.

She rubbed her coat against them, polishing it so it shone like the brightest silver. Then she stood up and gave herself a shake.

She was just about to search for a puddle to check her reflection, when she heard a buzzing noise from somewhere above her head.

'Zzzzzz!'

It was *very* loud. Paige paused, her ears pricked.

'Pleazzze, pleazzze, can you help uzzz?'

Who could that be? And where was it coming from?

CHAPTER TWO

A Sticky Problem

The buzzing noise was getting

even louder. 'Pleazzze help uzzz,

Petal Pony!'

Paige craned her silvery neck

and looked up. High in a tree, in

among the branches, there was a huge swarm of bees, hovering.

Paige came to Heather Hill every day to swish her tail over the flowers, and she often met the bees flying about to gather pollen. But she'd never seen them in a huge swarm like this. They seemed to be very upset about something.

'Hello, bees,' she said politely. 'Is something wrong?'

'Yezzz! they buzzed. 'Can you help uzzz?'

'Of course,' Paige said. 'I'm getting ready for the Pony Gala. But I don't mind helping.'

One of the bees swooped down to Paige. 'Thank you so much! It'zzz our honeycomb. We've been so busy making honey for the fairy animalzzz to eat at the Gala tonight . . .'

'Yum,' Paige said. 'Honey!'

'. . . but the honeycomb'zzz stuck inside the tree and we can't lift it out,' the bee finished. 'Pleazzze help!'

Paige looked up at the tree.

There was a big hole in the trunk.
'Is it in there?' she said, swishing
at the hole with her tail.

'Yezzz,' the bee said.

Paige fluttered her wings and
flew up on to a branch next to the
hole. She poked her nose inside.
Down at the bottom she could
see a big honeycomb, oozing with
golden honey. But she couldn't
reach it.

Beating her wings gently,

A STICKY PROBLEM

Paige poked her hoof inside
the hole and tried to ease
the honeycomb out. But the
honeycomb wouldn't budge.

'It's stuck,' she told the bees.

The bees trembled with
disappointment. 'Oh no,' they
buzzed. 'What a dizzzazzzter!'

'Don't worry,' Paige said. 'I'll
just try a bit harder.'

She poked her hoof in again
and tried to push the honeycomb

a little more. But it still wouldn't shift. Paige fluttered her wings and pushed her hoof against it with all her might.

A moment later, the honeycomb came unstuck from the hole with a large *PLOP!*

'Huzzzah!' buzzed the bees.

Paige pushed her hoof a little more against the honeycomb, trying to ease it through the hole. With a sudden squelch, the

31

honeycomb shot out into the air.

Paige was so surprised that she let go. She fell off the branch and tumbled on to a heather bush.

Before she had time to blink, the huge honeycomb came whizzing after her.

Slurp! It landed on her back and smashed into pieces.

'Oh no,' Paige cried, as the honey trickled down her sides. 'It's broken!'

32

'Doezzzn't matter,' the bees
buzzed. 'There's loadzzz of lovely
honey inside the pieces. There'll

be lots and lots for the fairy
animalzzz to eat. Thank you!'

The bees flew over and lifted
the pieces of honeycomb from
Paige's back.

'You've been so kind,' they
buzzed. 'Now it'zzz eazzzy for
uzzz to carry. See you at the
Gala, Paige!'

And they flew off towards
Misty Wood, each bee carrying a
chunk of honeycomb.

34

'Goodbye, bees,' Paige said,

relieved she'd been able to help.

Then the little petal pony looked round at her coat. A moment ago it had been so beautifully shiny. Now it was covered in sticky trails of honey.

She licked her shoulders, enjoying the yummy taste of the honey. She tried to lick her back and her sides, too, but she couldn't reach.

Then she tried rolling in the heather again, but instead of

making her coat nice and shiny,
all the twigs and leaves on the
ground got stuck to the honey!

What a mess I am, Paige
thought sadly, looking at her
sticky, twiggy coat. *How can I
clean up in time for the Gala?*

She hung her head, and her
snowy mane fluttered over her
eyes in the sunshine.

Then Paige had a brighter
thought. *If my mane looks really*

soft, maybe the judges won't notice my sticky coat!

She trotted off into the forest again, her little ears pricked. All she had to do was find somebody who could comb out her mane for her, and make it look really beautiful. Then she'd be ready for the Prettiest Pony Competition!

CHAPTER THREE

Birthday Blues

Paige hadn't gone very far into the wood when a black-and-white stripy face popped out from behind a tree. It was a young Bark Badger.

*Just the fairy animal I need
to help me with my mane,* Paige
thought. She trotted over and
gave a friendly flick of her head.

'Hello there,' she said politely.
'Could you help me get ready
for the Gala? I'm entering the
Prettiest Pony competition and I
need to look shiny and soft and
silky and bright. You've got such
long claws – they'd be perfect for
combing my mane.'

40

The bark badger shook her head. 'I'm sorry,' she sniffled. 'I can't.' She looked very unhappy.

A tear welled up and slid down her furry cheek.

'What's wrong?' Paige said softly. 'My name's Paige, by the way.'

'I'm Bessie,' the badger said, wiping the tear away. 'And I'm a very bad Bark Badger.'

'You don't look bad to me,' Paige said, shaking her head. 'You look very kind.'

The little badger sighed.

'It's my mum's birthday today, and I haven't got her a present. I want to give her one, but I can't think what to make! She'll be so disappointed.'

'Hmm,' Paige said thoughtfully. 'That is a pickle.'

She remembered the lovely present that her mum and dad had given her for her last birthday. They knew apples were Paige's favourite treat, so they'd

43

made a big hay-and-apple cake.

'Bessie, has your mum got
a favourite thing?' Paige asked.
'Something she really likes?'

Bessie wrinkled her nose, deep
in thought. 'Yes, she does,' she
said, after a moment. 'Mum loves
leaves. Silver leaves and golden
leaves, and yellowy-greeny ones,
too. Oh, and red ones, of course.
Especially red ones. Red is her
favourite colour.'

Paige gave a little skip. 'Perfect!' she said. 'I've got a brilliant idea, Bessie. Let's make a basket for your mum, and fill it with the brightest, prettiest leaves we can find. What do you think?'

Bessie clapped her paws. 'That would be the best present!'

'You collect some twigs to make the basket,' Paige said. 'You'll be really good at that, because you're a Bark Badger.

And I'll hunt for the prettiest
leaves I can find.'

'You're so kind,' Bessie said.
'Thank you!' She trundled off to
find the twigs.

Paige flicked her wings and
fluttered to the tree tops, where
masses of leaves whispered in the
breeze.

This should be easy, she
thought. *There must be millions of
leaves up here.*

But because it was summer, most of the leaves were green. Paige had to fly a long way before she found a tree with silver leaves like shining coins.

She gathered lots of them and tucked them safely into her tail. Then she spotted a tall tree with yellowy-greeny leaves that looked like feathers. She collected lots of those, too.

Bessie's present will be amazing,

she thought. *But I must find some golden leaves, too.*

Down below, there was a clump of bushes with tiny leaves like drops of gold. Paige swooped

down and picked as many as she

could to add to her collection.

Then she remembered that

Bessie's mum's favourite colour

was red. And she hadn't found

any red leaves at all.

But then she spotted a beautiful crimson leaf, hanging right in the middle of the bushes. 'That's it!' Paige said aloud. 'Perfect!'

She squeezed in through the bushes, ignoring the twigs as they tugged at her mane. She pushed on through the prickly branches until she had caught the red leaf in her teeth. Then she tried to turn back.

But she couldn't move. Her
mane was tangled and twisted in
the sharp twigs!

'Uh-oh,' she said. 'Help! I'm
stuck!'

After a moment, she heard
someone padding over to the
bushes.

'Hello, Paige. Look what I've
made!' Bessie came hurrying up,
carrying a little basket. 'Oh, what
are you doing in there?'

PAIGE THE PONY

'I'm stuck,' Paige said, embarrassed. She couldn't turn her head, or the twigs would pull on her mane. 'I've got all tangled up in this bush and I can't move at all!'

'Don't panic,' Bessie said. 'I'll have you free in a minute.' She grabbed the bush and snapped off the twigs until Paige was free.

'Phew!' Paige said, shaking herself out. 'Thank you, Bessie.

Oh – and these are for your mum.' She swished her tail, and the bright leaves fell in a pile.

'They're lovely,' Bessie said, jumping up and down, clapping her paws together. 'You're so clever, Paige.'

Bessie put the leaves in her basket. First the greeny-yellow ones, then the ones like silver coins, then the golden ones – and finally the red leaf, right on top.

BIRTHDAY BLUES

'What a beautiful basket you've made,' said Paige admiringly. 'And the leaves are so bright! Your mum will love her present.'

'Thank you so much, Paige,' Bessie said, giving her new friend a hug. 'Good luck at the Pony Gala.'

Bessie looked delighted as she hurried off to give the birthday gift to her mum.

Feeling happy herself, Paige called goodbye to Bessie and set off along a narrow path through the forest. It made her feel good, helping other fairy animals.

But as Paige trotted along, she felt something scratching against her neck. The broken-off twigs were still tangled up in her mane. *Oh no,* she thought. *My mane looks even worse now!*

Paige was feeling very

worried. How could she enter the Prettiest Pony Competition when she was such a mess? She didn't want everyone to laugh at her.

Down by the path, a little white flower was growing. It looked like a bright star against the dark soil. Paige stopped to look at it.

'Wait a minute!' she said to herself. 'I'm really good at collecting things. Why don't I find

58

lots of pretty flowers and make myself a garland? I can hang it round my neck and then no one will notice my tangled mane.'

Feeling pleased, Paige twirled her wings and darted off towards Honeydew Meadow. That was where the best flowers grew!

CHAPTER FOUR
Help, We're Lost!

Paige flitted through the trees.
She had to hurry. It was a long
way to Honeydew Meadow, and
it would take her ages to weave a
garland.

Soon her shimmering fairy wings began to feel tired. *I'd better trot for a while,* she thought.

She drifted down towards a green path that wound its way through the tree trunks. As her hoofs touched the ground, she heard a funny squeaking noise.

Paige pricked her ears and kept very still. The noise was coming from deep in the forest.

It sounds like someone crying,

61

the little pony thought. *I'd better go and see if I can help.* She stepped off the path towards the sound.

Paige had never been right into the Heart of Misty Wood before. It was shady and cool here, and the trees grew close together. The ground was muddy and her hoofs sank deep into the puddles. But someone was in trouble, and she had to help them.

'Hello?' she called softly.

'Who's there?'

'It's us,' a tiny voice mewed.

'We're lost!'

Paige hurried towards the
voice. There, right in the middle of
the forest, she saw a Bud Bunny
and a Cobweb Kitten, huddled
together on top of a log.

'Bella and Chloe!' Paige said,

surprised. 'What are you doing?'

'We were playing h-h-hide-and-seek,' Bella the Bud Bunny explained in a shaky voice. 'I was looking for the best hiding place and I hopped all the way here.

I waited for Chloe to find me. But
it was so scary . . .'

'It took me ages to find Bella,'
Chloe said, her lip trembling.

'And then . . .' Bella's long
ears drooped. 'We realised we
were lost.'

'So we thought we'd wait
until someone came,' Chloe
sniffled. 'But we waited for ages,
and nobody did! It was horrible.'

The two little friends looked

so miserable. Paige had to think
of something to cheer them up.
She tossed her head and gave a
little prance.

'It's all right!' she said. '*I'm*
here now. Jump on my back! I'll
give you a ride.'

'Oh, goody,' Bella said
gratefully, shaking her ears and
bounding onto Paige's back.

'Watch out for the honey,'
Paige said. 'I'm a bit sticky.'

'Don't worry, we love honey!'
Bella said. 'Honey's yummy.'

Chloe climbed up Paige's tail
and sat beside Bella. 'Mind the
twigs in my mane!' Paige added.

'Don't scratch yourselves.'

'Don't worry, we'll use them
to hang on to!' The kitten tucked
her paws round one of the twigs.

'Ready? Off we go!' Paige
called as she cantered away.

'Yay,' shouted Bella, her tears
forgotten. 'This is great!'

'Oh, yes,' squeaked Chloe.
'I love riding on a fairy pony!'

Paige's plan to make a
flowery garland slipped right out

of her mind. Instead, she pranced
in little circles around the trees.

'Whoopee!' yelled Bella.
'You're so bouncy, Paige.'

Then Paige saw a branch
lying across the path. She
galloped up and leapt over. Then
she jumped it the other way.

'Ooooh,' squealed Chloe,
clinging on tight to Paige's mane.
'You're a brilliant jumper!'

'How about this?' Paige said,

and twirled round in a pirouette.

'Wheeeeee!' squeaked
Bella. 'You should go in the
showjumping at the Pony Gala!'

'Oh yes, you'll be wonderful,'
Chloe agreed.

Paige stopped spinning. 'Oh
no!' she gasped. 'I forgot all about
the Prettiest Pony Competition.
I'm supposed to be getting all
shiny and soft and silky and
bright, but I'm all tangled and

sticky and matted and muddy!'

'I know,' Bella said. 'Why
don't you drop us off at Moonshine Pond, where you can have
a bath? We know the way home
from there.'

'That's a great idea,' Paige
said, relieved.

She set off through Misty
Wood at her fastest gallop, with
her two friends clinging on tightly
to the twigs in her mane.

When they got to Moonshine Pond, Bella and Chloe jumped down from Paige's back. 'See you at the Gala!' Bella called.

'We hope you win the competition,' Chloe added.

'Thank you!' Paige said.

As she headed over to the water, she glanced up and saw that the sun was starting to drop down above the treetops. There was no time to lose!

CHAPTER FIVE

Hunting for Hazelnuts

Before Paige could dip into the water, she caught sight of something red and fluffy darting around in the bushes. It looked

like a tail. But whose tail?

Forgetting the water for a moment, Paige trotted closer to have a look. The tail was wriggling about, as if it was attached to someone who was very busy indeed.

Suddenly the tail was gone, and a face with two beady brown eyes popped up in its place.

A Stardust Squirrel!

'Hello,' the squirrel said, with

a worried look in his eyes. 'I'm Sammy.'

'I'm Paige,' the Petal Pony replied. 'Is everything all right?'

'No,' the squirrel replied in a very serious voice. 'Everything is not all right. In fact everything is all *wrong*!'

'Oh dear,' Paige said. 'What's happened?'

'I've lost something VERY important indeed. Ah – hold on!'

Sammy darted towards a clump of grass. 'Maybe this is the place!'

He started digging. Soon he had dug such a deep hole that Paige could only see his back legs and tail. Then Sammy wriggled out again, with a blob of dirt on the end of his nose.

'Nothing!' he said. 'This is terrible. Worse than terrible.' He looked at Paige and twitched his nose. 'What's worse than terrible?'

HUNTING FOR HAZELNUTS

'Er, horrible?' Paige said.

'Yes, it's terrible and horrible – terri-horrible,' Sammy announced. 'I wonder – would you be very kind and help me? If you helped me we might find them and then this *wouldn't* be the worst day of my life ever.'

'Of course!' Paige said. 'But what are you looking for?'

Sammy had started digging again. Earth and stones flew up

like a fountain behind his busy paws. 'My *hazelnuts*, of course!' he said. 'I buried them last autumn. Right here, on the bank of Moonshine Pond. And now I can't find a single one.'

He scratched his head, looking very puzzled. 'I've *got* to find them. My friends and I are going to the Pony Gala this evening and we're supposed to be having a picnic. But we won't

have anything to eat if I can't find my hazelnuts.'

'I'm going to the Pony Gala, too,' Paige said, suddenly remembering what she was *supposed* to be doing. 'I'm in the Prettiest Pony Competition.'

'Oh.' Sammy sat back on his hind legs and looked her up and down.

'I know I look really messy,' Paige told him, feeling

embarrassed. 'But every time I try to make myself look prettier something happens to make me even messier!'

'Well – your tail looks very pretty!' Sammy said. 'It's so long and silky and white.'

'Thank you!' Paige said, and felt better. Poor Sammy – he was so worried about his picnic. Surely it wouldn't take long to find a few hazelnuts?

'How can I help?' she asked.

'Well,' Sammy said, 'those hoofs of yours would be great for digging.'

Paige nodded her head. 'They are. Do you have any idea where your hazelnuts might be buried?'

'No,' Sammy said sadly. 'It was somewhere on the bank, but I just don't know *where*.'

Paige thought for a moment. 'My mum loses things sometimes.

84

Like our apples. She hides them under the hedge, or behind a tree trunk, to keep them safe, and then she can't find them. "I put those apples in a very safe place," she says, "And now I can't remember where that safe place is!"'

Sammy nodded. 'That's just like me. My hazelnuts are very precious indeed. I always look for a safe place to hide them.'

'Well, maybe what we

need to do is to look all around
Moonshine Pond for the safest
place,' Paige suggested. 'I bet
your hazelnuts will be there.'

'Good idea!' exclaimed
Sammy. 'What about under
those tree roots?'

Paige followed
him to a big tree
near the pond. She
scraped the earth
away with

her hoofs, but there were no hazelnuts hidden under the roots.

'What about those reeds by the water?' Paige said. 'Maybe you hid the hazelnuts between the stems.'

'Good thinking!' Sammy cried, and the two of them rummaged around among the reeds, but still they couldn't find the hazelnuts.

'This is hopeless,' Sammy

groaned. 'We'll never
be able to have our
picnic.'

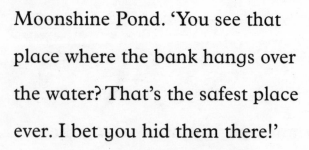

'Wait a minute.'
Paige looked across at
Moonshine Pond. 'You see that
place where the bank hangs over
the water? That's the safest place
ever. I bet you hid them there!'

She cantered over to the very
edge of the Pond.

'Careful!' Sammy called,

88

scampering along. 'Don't fall in!'

It was hard, leaning over
and digging at the bank with her
hoofs. But Paige knew it was the
best place to find the hazelnuts.

And sure enough, there they
were – lots of tasty brown nuts,
gently wrapped in leaves to keep
them clean, tucked away right
inside the bank.

'Sammy, I've found them!'
Paige called. But she was so

excited that she slipped on the
muddy bank and lost her balance.
'Help!' she squealed, as she slid
towards the squelchy brown mud.

Sammy fluttered up and grabbed her mane in his teeth. 'Steady!' he said. 'I've got you.'

Paige clambered back onto the grass.

'Thank you, you're so kind!' Sammy chattered, as he gathered up the hazelnuts one by one. 'This is going to be the best picnic ever! See you at the Gala, Paige! Good luck!'

And he rolled up the nuts in

91

a water lily leaf and rushed off to find his friends.

Paige went to wave goodbye to him with her tail, but it felt really heavy. 'Oh no,' she cried as she looked over her shoulder. Her tail was soaking wet, and covered in chocolatey-brown mud.

'*Drrrrrrr! Drrrrrrr!*' A loud noise boomed through the wood.

Paige pricked her ears. The woodpeckers were drumming a

message on the tree trunks. The Pony Gala was about to begin!

She looked down at her reflection on the smooth surface of the pond.

I look messier that ever! she thought. Her coat was sticky. Her mane had twigs in it. Her hoofs were muddy – and now her tail was, too!

High up in the sky there was a tweeting sound. Paige looked up

to see a beautiful bluebird flying
overhead.

'It's Gala time!' the bluebird
tweeted. 'Make your way to
Golden Meadow!'

I can't, Paige thought to herself sadly. *I'm just too messy and scruffy.* She would simply have to miss out on the Prettiest Pony Competition this year.

At least, she'd have to miss out on *entering* the competition.

I can still watch this year, I suppose, Paige thought sadly. *I just need to find a good spot to see from, where nobody will see me.*

CHAPTER SIX
A Very Special Prize

Paige peeped out from behind
a mossy tree trunk at the edge
of Golden Meadow. It was the
perfect hiding spot for a little

Petal Pony, right behind the
judges' panel for the Prettiest
Pony Competition. She could see
everything, but she was pretty
sure no one could see her.

The showjumping had just finished. The winner was Pippin, a pony with a coat like a shiny brown conker. Paige's dad was presenting the prize to him – a huge cake made of apples and heather.

'Yippeee!' cheered all the ponies that were watching. 'Great win, Pippin!'

'Yay, well done!' shouted all the fairy animals in the crowd.

Paige wished she could join in with the shouting and cheering. But she was too shy to go anywhere near the Pony Gala when she looked such a state.

Then she heard a familiar little whinny. Her baby sister Pia was trotting across the Meadow, right near Paige's hiding spot.

Pia looked so cute, with her mane and tail as fluffy as a dandelion clock. Paige wanted to

go and rub noses with her, but she
couldn't leave the tree trunk.

'Daddy! Have you seen
Paige?' Paige heard Pia ask.

'No, I haven't,' their dad
replied. 'It's nearly time for the
Prettiest Pony Competition, and
we don't want her to miss out!

Let's see if we can find her.'

Paige's heart skipped a beat.
But then the two of them trotted
away towards the crowd. Her
hiding place was safe.

In the middle of the Meadow,
a team of Cobweb Kittens was
stretching a rope of cobwebs
into a big circle for the Prettiest
Pony Competition. They hung
shimmering dewdrops all along it.

Beautiful Petal Ponies began

trotting into the ring, their silky manes and tails floating in the air. Their eyes shone with excitement as the crowd started cheering. Paige caught sight of her friend Poppy, her blue wings sparkling in the sunlight.

Little Pia cantered up to the judges' panel. 'You have to stop the competition,' she squeaked at the judges. 'Paige is missing and we can't find her anywhere.'

'Oh dear,' said one of the judges, a regal brown pony with white patches. 'We can't keep everyone waiting. Do you know where she is?'

Paige's mum hurried across the ring. 'Perhaps she's just forgotten . . .'

Pia shook her head. 'Paige wouldn't forget. She's been looking forward to it all summer.'

Paige's friend Poppy trotted

104

over, looking confused. 'Where is
Paige? She said she'd be here.'

Then Pia began to cry.
'Where is she?'

Paige couldn't bear to see her
baby sister so upset. She took a
deep breath and leapt out from
her hiding spot.

'I'm here,' she said softly,
cantering over to the judges.

'Hooray!' Pia said, rushing
over to rub noses with Paige as

Poppy sighed with relief.

Pia didn't seem to notice her sticky coat and tangled mane and muddy hoofs and slimy tail. 'I'm so glad you're all right,' Pia whispered.

The other judge, a coal-black pony, tossed her mane importantly. 'Now that all our contestants are here,' she said, 'we may begin the Prettiest Pony Competition!'

As the two judges called all the ponies into the ring, Paige turned to her mum and Pia. 'I'm still not ready,' she told them fretfully.

'You always look beautiful to

me,' her mum said, nuzzling her. 'Now go out there and show them how pretty you are, on the inside and out!'

Paige took a deep breath, and trotted into the ring with Poppy and the other ponies. She arched her neck, and skipped around, and kicked her heels in the air. Pretty soon, she was having so much fun that she'd forgotten about how messy she looked.

A VERY SPECIAL PRIZE

In the crowd, she could see Petey the Puppy, and Daisy the Deer, and Mia the Mouse. They were all waving and smiling at her. Everyone was watching, but Paige didn't mind.

This is so much fun, she thought, as she did a perfect pirouette. *Who cares if I'm scruffy and messy? I'm just glad to be here with Poppy and Pia and all these beautiful ponies.*

When the judges were ready to announce their winner, the ponies stopped prancing and the crowd burst into applause. The Petal Ponies stood still, beaming, as the black pony judge stepped forward. The crowd fell silent.

'This has been a particularly exciting year for the Prettiest Pony Competition,' the judge said. 'And we'd like to congratulate the winner, a

111

beautiful young pony by the name of . . .'

Paige held her breath. She couldn't win – could she?

'. . . Poppy!' the judge finished, and the crowd went wild.

Paige cheered just as loudly as everyone else, delighted for her friend. She hardly minded that she hadn't won, because Poppy was indeed a very beautiful pony, and a very good friend as well.

The judges pinned a red rosette to Poppy's mane and presented her with her prize – a huge cake made of carrots and honey. Poppy's golden coat shone, and her hoofs were as bright as pearly shells. She deserved to win the prize.

Everyone cheered and clapped as Poppy trotted around prettily with her honey and carrot cake. Paige and the other ponies

cantered out of the ring to watch.

As Paige stood there on the sidelines, she heard a loud buzzing noise. A swarm of bees was flying across the ring – coming straight towards her! They were carrying a piece of honeycomb, shaped just like a flower, which they laid carefully on Paige's head. It smelled lovely.

'This izzz to say thank you for being so kind,' they buzzed.

Then Bessie the Badger came lolloping over the grass, carrying a comb made from birch bark. 'You were so kind, Paige,' she said. 'Thank you for helping me make Mum's present – she really likes it. I've made you a comb for your mane!'

'It was no trouble,' Paige told them. 'I enjoyed helping.'

She lowered her head so that Bessie could comb away the twigs

115

and tangles. Then Bessie fixed the comb in Paige's mane, just behind the honeycomb flower.

Then Chloe and Bella hurried over. Chloe had a big basket with her, and Bella was carrying a garland of pink and blue flowers.

'I hope we're not too late,' Chloe mewed, as she sprinkled dewdrops from the basket over Paige's coat and rubbed until all the sticky honey was gone.

A VERY SPECIAL PRIZE

Then she washed Paige's muddy hoofs so they were shiny again.

'Oh, that's lovely,' Paige said softly. She didn't tell Chloe the competition was over, and that Poppy had won. She didn't want to hurt her feelings.

Bella fluttered in the air and placed the flower garland around Paige's neck. 'Thanks for helping us,' she said. 'We'd never have got safely home without you.'

'You're welcome,' Paige said with a smile.

Then someone scampered up behind her. 'Hi there,' Sammy chirped, as he scattered sparkling stardust all over Paige's tail. 'I just had to come and say thank you for helping me find my hazelnuts – our picnic was delicious!'

A big cheer went up from all the Stardust Squirrels in the crowd. Paige looked up, and

realised that the other fairy animals had gone silent.

Everyone was looking over at her curiously, including Poppy, who'd finished her winner's circuit.

'There,' Sammy said, when he'd finished. 'You really are the prettiest pony now.'

Paige blushed, suddenly feeling shy. The two judges came over to see what was happening.

'What beautiful decorations!'

the regal brown pony said,
looking closely at the honey
flower and the bark comb.

'Indeed!' The black pony
nodded, admiring the garland
and the shimmering stardust.
'It's a shame the competition is
over. You look very pretty, Paige!'

'Oh no,' mewed Chloe. 'We
were too late!'

'I'm sorry,' said Bella, her
ears drooping.

121

'Me too,' said Bessie.

'Oh, no,' Sammy sighed.

'Dizzzaster,' buzzed the bees.
'We should have come faster!'

But the black pony shook
her head. 'We couldn't help
overhearing what your friends
were saying,' she said. 'And
being kind is just as important as
being pretty. So we've decided to
award you a very special prize.
Congratulations, Paige, for being

the Kindest Pony in Misty Wood!'
Then she pinned a beautiful red
rosette onto Paige's mane, and
gave her a basket filled with red
apples.

'Ooh,' Paige said. She was so
happy she could hardly speak!
She squeaked out, 'Thank you!'
Then she realised the crowd
around them had been watching,
and now they were cheering.

'Hooray, Paige! Well done,

Paige!' roared the crowd, as she beamed and tossed her silky mane.

★

Later that afternoon, after the Gala was over, Paige and her family stood under a shady tree and shared the apples as the sun went down.

'I'm so proud of you,' Pia said, cuddling up to Paige.

Paige's dad swished his tail happily. 'So am I!' he said. 'You entered the competition even though

126

you hadn't had time to get ready.
You knew you wouldn't win, but
you still took part.'

'You're the Kindest Pony,'
Paige's mum said, 'and that
makes me the proudest mum! Well
done, Paige.'

Paige felt all warm and happy inside. She thought of the friends she had helped today, and how they had helped her, too.

'I just did what any good fairy animal would do,' she said happily, and crunched into one of the delicious red apples.

Turn the page for lots of fun Misty Wood activities!

Spot the difference

The picture on the opposite page is slightly different to this one. Can you circle all the differences?

MAZE

Help Paige get to the Prettiest Pony competition and win the prize apples!

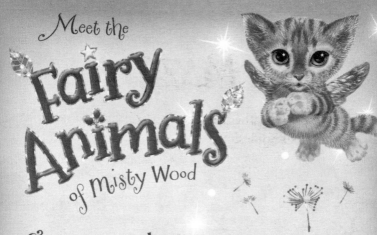

Meet the

Fairy Animals
of Misty Wood

There's a whole world to explore!

Download the FREE *Fairy Animals* app and visit **fairyanimals.com** for lots of gorgeous goodies . . .

- ✷ Free stuff
- ✷ Games
- ✷ Write to your favourite characters
- ✷ Step inside Misty Wood
- ✷ Send us your cute pet pictures
- ✷ Make your own fairy wings!

Fairy Animals

of Misty Wood

Meet all the fairy animal friends!

Lily Small — Chloe the Kitten — **Fairy Animals** of Misty Wood

Lily Small — Bella the Bunny — **Fairy Animals** of Misty Wood

Lily Small — Paddy the Puppy — **Fairy Animals** of Misty Wood

Lily Small — Mia the Mouse — **Fairy Animals** of Misty Wood

Lily Small — Hailey the Hedgehog — **Fairy Animals** of Misty Wood

Lily Small — Poppy the Pony — **Fairy Animals** of Misty Wood

Lily Small — Sophie the Squirrel — **Fairy Animals** of Misty Wood

Lily Small — Betsy the Bunny — **Fairy Animals** of Misty Wood

Lily Small — Daisy the Deer — **Fairy Animals** of Misty Wood

Lily Small — Kylie the Kitten — **Fairy Animals** of Misty Wood

Lily Small — Polly the Puppy — **Fairy Animals** of Misty Wood

Lily Small — Paige the Pony — **Fairy Animals** of Misty Wood